Payback with My Boyfriend's Dad

FORBIDDEN FERTILE AGE GAP

TAKING HER INNOCENCE

CANDY QUINN

PATHFORGERS PUBLISHING

© 2024 Pathforgers Publishing

All Rights Reserved. This is a work of fiction. This book is intended for sale to Adult Audiences only. All characters depicted in this work of fiction are 18 years of age or older. All sexual activity is between non-blood related, consenting adults.

Contents

Preface — v

Payback with My Boyfriend's Dad — 1

Recommended For You — 25
Free Exclusive Story — 27
Become Candy Obsessed — 31

Preface

Sign up to my newsletter to receive free, exclusive stories:
http://candyquinn.com/newsletter

Book Themes: virgin, age gap, older man/younger woman, boyfriend's dad, breeding, bareback
Word Count: 5169

Payback with My Boyfriend's Dad

The Mediterranean sun approached its peak, and its golden rays glistened as they hit my oiled body. Even though I was slathered in sunscreen to protect my youthful skin, a tan was still developing.

I looked down, over the hills of my breasts, down the valley to my thighs, and smiled.

It was nice to feel lazy and relaxed.

My boyfriend, Russ, had finally invited me on a family vacation, and the island was practically deserted. Still, I wore a gold bikini. Russ and I hadn't gone all the way yet, and I didn't want him to think that bringing me on vacation was a free pass for my body.

I had more self respect than that.

Besides, it was his dad's house.

My eyes closed beneath my sunglasses, and I relaxed on the chaise, enjoying the peace.

A sudden splash of a thick, syrupy liquid between my breasts shocked me out of it.

"Ah!"

I startled, pushing myself up on the chaise, just as a sticky and creamy combination of pineapple juice and coconut milk covered my tits and torso. It slid down my stomach until it was running rivulets between my thighs.

"Russ!"

He stared down at me without an ounce of apology. His gaze was focused on where the drink had spilled, lust clear in his eyes.

"You did that on purpose!"

I jumped up, staring at him with unbridled rage.

Russ had a lot of things going for him—his wealth, his good looks, his confidence—but little of it had to do with his personality.

Instead of telling me it was an accident, he just shrugged a shoulder, smirking. "I'll clean it up with my tongue if you want."

My face tightened.

"Jackass," I said, throwing the lounge pillow at him as I pushed past. "I'm getting a shower."

His eyes burned into me as I walked away.

He had been giving me a rough time over not putting out for a while now, and I kept telling him to prove he was committed to me. This vacation was supposed to be how he did that, but he seemed intent on giving himself a permanent case of blue balls at this rate.

"Woah, what happened, Lacey?"

From out of the sliding glass door came Russ's father, Maximus. Even though his outfit comprised casual linen, a button-down shirt and complimentary shorts, he was refined. It was carefully tailored, and the gold watch and chocolate-brown boat shoes were perfect accessories.

A complete opposite to Russ's graphic print tee-shirt and ill-fitted board shorts.

"Oh! Mr. Calihan. Your son thinks he's funny. He is not." I flicked some of my downy blonde hair off my shoulder, my cheeks still red with anger. "Now I get to spend the afternoon showering off sugar and washing out my bathing suit instead of enjoying the sun."

"That little—" his father began, biting his tongue, literally it appeared. "You know, he tried that same thing on one of the maids before?" He shook his head with absolute disgust.

"I'm so sorry, sweetie. I know it does nothing for you now, but... I'll treat you to a couple replacement sets next time we're near a shop," he offered in condolences. His expression was at once apologetic and dashing.

I did a double-take.

Russ would tell me to get them laundered, and accuse me of over-reacting.

My expression journeyed from confusion to disbelief, before finally setting on appreciation.

"I might take you up on that," I laughed.

By the time I got to my bedroom, I had calmed down a little.

Maybe I was wrong, and it had been an accident, and Russ was just trying to act cool to cover it up.

I doubted it, but I was on vacation for the next ten days. I didn't want to spend all that time stewing.

The shower was bigger than my apartment's entire bathroom, and the water almost felt too clean. Too pure. It was water for the rich, somehow better than *normal* water. I stepped under it, letting the steam ease my aches. The stickiness between my chest drained away, and I traced a hand down between my breasts, chasing away the rest.

Mirrored tile surrounded me, and I watched my hands caress my nubile skin. My breasts were perky, and everything beneath my eyebrows had been waxed to prepare for the trip. I glided further down, still tingling with sensitivity as I touched my mons. It was strange being so smooth, and I couldn't help but tease my finger against my clit, grinning at my reflection.

Bad girl, I chastised myself. *Hurry up and get back outside to enjoy the sun.*

I showered, the body wash and hair products all fabulously decadent. By the time I finished, I still smelled sweet, but I didn't feel sticky any longer. I stepped out, only then realizing I hadn't taken the time to grab a towel.

"Crap."

Looking beneath the sink and in the cupboards, I found things well stocked, but not with towels.

I guess the maid hadn't restocked the bathroom yet.

I found a hand towel, and I grabbed that, doing my best to pat myself dry.

The bathroom was shared between my room and Russ's. There were no towels on my side that I'd found, so I opened up the other door to check his.

A gasp died in my throat.

Russ was on his bed, but he wasn't alone. I couldn't get a good look at her face, since he was pressing it into the pillows as he plowed into her from behind. Neither of them heard my intrusion, and in my shock, I stepped back into the bathroom, silently closing the door.

I sprinted back into my room, only belatedly noticing that I'd dropped the hand towel at some point. I paced, my head spinning. For a moment, I thought I might faint.

My boyfriend was cheating on me.

How had he even *found* someone to fuck?

It was a quick shower!

I couldn't have been gone for more than a half hour.

It had to be staff.

The only other people in the vacation manor were me and his dad. And he hadn't even locked the door!

I was so mad that it wasn't until I instinctively raised a hand to block the sun from my eyes that I realized I'd been pacing, naked, in front of the floor-to-ceiling windows. Mr. Calihan was in the pool, and when I caught his gaze, he waved at me. His tanned, muscular body was partially submerged, but the sun cast attractive shadows over his strong jaw and broad shoulders.

All that rage, all that anger, all bubbled up in me.

I had been planning to give my virginity to Russ on the vacation, despite my playing coy.

Now I had a better idea.

"Fuck it."

I stomped out of the room, not even bothering to throw on a cover-up, and didn't stop until I was standing, naked, at the edge of the pool. I looked at Mr. Calihan, my pale eyes still burning with jealous, embarrassed, righteous anger.

"Your son is a shit."

Mr. Calihan rose out of the pool, water cascading over his sculpted, older body. He ran a hand back over his hair, pushing it from his ruggedly handsome face. He was a man who had worked for his wealth, at least.

You could tell just by looking at him.

And as he looked me over, he didn't appear shocked at my nudity. Not quite. It was as if he thought I was making some artistic statement.

"What the hell did he do now?" he asked, some gravel in his voice. I felt the irritation in him rising, much as he was moving through the water, rising out of it more with each step as he approached me.

"You said he tried that move on one of the maids before?" My tongue was acidic, the heat from the sun positively chilly compared to my righteous fury.

Mr. Calihan exited the pool, his towering body standing over me, glistening in the Mediterranean sun.

"Yeah. She's still with us, though I don't know why. I paid her for the trouble and apologized, but..." He shook his head, his steely eyes sweeping over me. "I can understand why the boy is so smitten with you, but that's no excuse for being a sleaze. I don't know where I went wrong with that one," he said, wetting his full, peachy lower lip.

"You want anything?" he asked, reaching over for a towel, and unfurling it, offering to wrap me up in it.

I was too angry, though, and swatted it away.

"He's in his room fucking someone as we speak," I spat out. "We've barely been here three hours, and I was gone for like *two seconds* before he was balls deep in her. I *really* doubt this is the first time he's cheated on me, but it is definitely the last."

I could see Mr. Calihan's eyes widen at what I'd just told him. He was a rich man, a very rich man. But he upheld himself with some class and respectability, unlike his son.

"He's *what?!*" he asked sharply, looking up at the upper level of the manor, appearing ready to storm up there and rip his son off the help. I could see veins on his forearm and biceps bulge as he clenched his fists. "I should have beaten his ass to teach him a lesson years ago!" he growled.

A shiver went through me. It felt so *good* to have someone on my side. To feel his anger radiating out of him, just as righteous and unhinged as mine. My breath caught in my chest, and the noise I made was a cross between a giggle and a moan.

It was funny, in a way. Hearing him uphold and mirror my anger was the balm that soothed it, and it was then that I could actually see the humour in the situation. There I was, standing naked in front of my soon-to-be-ex-boyfriend's dad. The vacation property was out of a magazine, with a cerulean sky dotted with wispy, white clouds. Luxury surrounded me.

And in front of me, I was seeing Mr. Calihan in a new light. His veins popped, his jaw clenched, his muscles perfectly highlighted in the hot sun.

My hand went to his left pec. My thumb caressed the skin, feeling the rugged hair beneath it. His heart was racing, just like mine.

"He's been giving me a hard time about being a virgin. That's why he took me on this vacation in the first place. I think he'll soon know how much he fucked up without you ever laying a hand on him. Especially if you decide to lay a hand on me instead."

Mr. Calihan was a handsome, rich, and powerful older man. There was no way I was the only hot young thing who made a pass at him. But when his gaze pulled away from the house to look at me, I felt like I was the only girl to have hit on him in ages.

His steely eyes swept across my petite form as he licked his lips.

Looking him over in return, it was impossible not to notice the wet material of his swimming shorts clinging to the outline of a partially turgid member.

"I'm not a pig like my son. I don't want to do something with you that you'll regret," he offered gentlemanly. But his voice dripped with desire all the same. He wasn't so much a gentleman that he was going to mask that desire. To take my proposal off the table entirely.

"Then make me not regret agreeing to spending ten days on a secluded island," I countered. "Your son will try to apologize, and I'll give in, and he'll keep pestering me for sex. I'm weak, Mr. Calihan. The only way that he won't get my virginity is if you take it first. Help me out. Let me get some payback. Show me how a real man would treat me."

Silence hung between us. But it wasn't awkward exactly. It was like we could both feel the buzz of attraction between us. The inevitability of that draw.

He took a deep breath, running a big hand back through his hair as he looked down at me.

"First of all," he began, licking his lips. "You're gonna be my girl for more than it takes to fuck you. It's over between my son and you, and as soon as we leave this island, I'm taking you out on a proper date. Like he's probably never done," he declared in his deep, rumbling voice.

And that was all enticing, but I was afraid he'd make me wait until then to pop my cherry.

I was wrong.

He reached out, putting his hand on my hip, drawing me closer.

"My room, or…?" he asked.

His acceptance was unexpected, despite my brazenness. Excitement churned my stomach, and my brain stopped working. It was a few heartbeats before I realized what he was saying, and then a few longer to process the question.

"Why not right here?"

Part of me just didn't want to give him time to change his mind. The other part of me?

God, I had to admit how much his possessiveness turned me on.

He was twice my age, but he was someone able to take care of me. Someone who wanted to do things for me.

To me.

The longer I stood next to him, the more I wanted to do things for him, too. He made me feel a way that Russ *never* did.

Russ was entitled. Mr. Calihan was confident. I was learning that there was a massive difference between those two things.

His hand, so big and strong, gripped my hip and his thumb caressed at my waist. He had such a powerful grasp, and as things spiralled between us, he pulled me closer.

"Just listen here," he said to me, his deep voice going lower as he brushed back some of my blonde hair with his other hand. He looked so serious, I might have thought he was about to talk me out of it. But instead, he said, "After this, I meant what I said. I want you to at least give us dating a try. I don't want us to just fuck, then forget about it. Got it?"

He was so firm and certain sounding. So in control, while I was almost feeling woozy from the dizzying excitement. But when he bent down and kissed my lips... that helped steady me. Anchoring me to the world via where our bodies touched.

I couldn't believe that *he* was worried that I might be using him. Maybe, when I first approached him, I was. He saw through that and called me out. But dating him seemed even more scandalous, and excitement danced beneath my flesh. My pussy throbbed in agreement, and I nodded, my upturned nose brushing against his as we kissed.

"I promise. I'll give it a try. Dating men my own age certainly hasn't been working out."

"Of course not," he said, caressing my cheek, plucking a few more moist kisses from my lips as he spoke to me so low and growly. "You're too beautiful. Too precious and unique to be appreciated by a boy."

We made out again, and he pulled me into his body. His cock throbbed against me.

"Little boys just want to conquer and move on. No appreciation for the finer aspects of life." His hands began to explore my body more aggressively, feeling up my breast with one hand. Not the fumbled, over-eager sort of groping that his son would do. He was careful not to get too rough, too greedy.

I'd never done something so bold as to stomp around naked, and I hadn't appreciated how vulnerable I was until he cupped by breast. A shock of desire struck through me, and I gasped. My nipple was already stiff, and my knees trembled.

Was I really doing this?

Was I really going to give my first time to a man just to get payback on his son?

His thumb and forefinger put pressure on my nipple, making it ache for more. He'd already given me more pleasure than Russ ever had. There was no resisting the fact that I wanted to go further. I'd arrived on the island ready to lose my virginity. It just would not happen with the man I thought it would.

Mr. Calihan had done his best to start off slowly, but the passion was rising. He wasn't a virgin, after all, not even close. And his desire was being let off its leash, until he was feeling me all over, almost crushing me against his hard, muscular body.

He groaned into my mouth as his cock grew big, throbbing against me.

"Fuck, I want you," he growled to me, sounding so possessive.

The sun was so hot, but what was growing between us was an inferno. My tongue teased his, tasted his words, and my hands trailed along his torso. I was shy about dipping lower, about finding his masculinity with my palm, despite my overwhelming desire to feel it. My upper thigh grazed it, and he throbbed at the attention.

"I can't wait. I need it," I gasped, shivering despite the warmth of the air.

Mr. Calihan dipped down, scooping my petite body up in one arm as we continued to kiss. He took me over to the ever so posh and expensive lounging seat by the side of the pool. He laid me down on it, and looking at me with a fierce, primal hunger in his eyes, he tugged his shorts off, letting his thick cock spring out.

"You're too hot to resist any longer anyhow."

He leaned down and began to kiss across my body, showering my breasts, my tummy, my mons with his oral affections.

I could only get a glimpse, but I was suddenly having a lot of second thoughts. Not because I didn't want him—I did. Not because he wasn't turning me on—he was.

But...

"That's too big to fit," I gasped belatedly, when he was already between my legs. My clarification was cut off by a moan as his tongue teased between my lips and my back arched intuitively.

He didn't respond to what I'd said, not with words at least.

Mr. Calihan was too smooth for that. He just assuaged me with his tongue on my most private of places, doing what his son would never have done: put aside his pleasure, to focus on mine.

And Mr. Calihan ate at my pussy like he was a starving man and I was the most delectable morsel he'd ever seen all at once. Only his movements were refined and aided by his self-control. He tongued my most sensitive of places, hoisting my smooth thighs up onto his shoulders as he got in there, tasting my honeyed arousal with full gusto.

The recent waxing had upped my sensitivity. My nerve endings were being teased so ruthlessly after being denied touch for so long. Every motion of his skilled tongue, every brush of his jaw or cheeks against my pussy lips, sent a jolt through me. For a moment, I forgot about everything else. About Russ, about how we were not in private, about the age difference, about the fact that I wasn't on the pill and we had no protection.

My orgasm was mightier than all else, and as it crashed over me, I heedlessly screamed, my hands balled into fists on either side of the lounge chair.

The way I was squirming and writhing must've looked absurd, or hot, I have no idea. Me thrusting my chest up and from side to side, making my perky little breasts jiggle and bounce. He kept tonguing me through that bliss though, until I was pushing my little fists to his shoulders, breathlessly gasping for him to stop.

He drew it on a moment longer, reminding me this big, strong, beautiful man was more than I could handle. But he was reserved, rising up, his cock rock solid as he wiped the back of his mouth and looked down at me with a feral hunger.

"You're gonna be a tight fit, for sure," he husked. He reached his hand down, one of his thick, masculine fingers stretching my little slit open as he tested my insides. But he wasn't dissuaded. His dick throbbed instead.

He'd rendered me brainless, and I stared at him dumbly. Fireworks still shot behind my eyes, and my balance shifted as if I were on a small ship. I rocked forward and back before deciding it was best not to move at all. Gasping in a long, hot breath, my blood was boiling, and I was dripping honey onto the lounge seat.

I couldn't even say anything. I just stared, wide-eyed, slack jawed, as he began to finger the opening of my pussy. It felt so good, despite my oversensitivity, and I mewled with animalistic need.

He silenced me with his lips, kissing me deep and passionately, while his finger began to tease and stretch open my little slit. It could've lasted an hour, or it could've been a few couple minutes, I have no idea. Everything was a blur by that point. I know I'd been moaning and mewling, squealing as a second finger got added.

"I can't wait anymore." He plucked his two fingers from my pussy, then put them into his mouth to suckle them clean. "Fuck, you're tasty," he rumbled.

I watched as this gorgeous, naked man grasped at his cock. He gave it a couple of pumps as he brought it down to my womanhood, teasing that enormous purple crown against my little pink vulva.

It was obscene. He was so much older than me, so much bigger. He had a rugged tan, and corded muscles that tensed as he held the position over me. Veins bulged in his forearms, and they pulsed to nearly the same tempo as the ones that ribbed his shaft.

He'd not mentioned a condom. Perhaps he assumed I was on the pill, since I'd been planning on giving my first to Russ. It didn't matter. I wasn't going to mention it, and neither was he. The raw risk just made it feel even more taboo. It made the revenge all that much sweeter.

We both watched with rapt attention, as my virgin little pussy went from such a soft pink hue to straining almost red as it stretched around his girth. I was straining to take him all in, and so far, it was just the head of his manhood that was penetrating me.

I was so lost in the moment I hadn't been aware I was squealing and screaming my head off. He slowly rocked his hips, stretching me open around his shaft.

"Fuck... fuck, you are too good for anyone else to have," he growled possessively as he released his cock. Having planted enough in me, he was no longer at risk of slipping away. But there was still so much more of that thick, veiny shaft to squeeze inside me.

It was exquisite pain, my young body sundered by his mature one. He awoke something carnal within me, and my brain went blissfully quiet as my lungs gave power to my screams. My spine curved, my head tilting back, and I damn near came again. Maybe I did. It was so intense, my virginal pussy resisting his intrusion, even as I gushed sweet juices all around his shaft.

And judging by the look on Mr. Calihan's face, the pleasure was by no means one-sided. He looked like he'd never felt such bliss, even as he tried to control himself, not to just grab me and begin pounding away without caring for my safety.

But soon he was thrusting all the way up inside me, filling me like I never thought was possible. Making me feel more whole than I imagined sex could.

"Fuck, that idiot never knew what he was missing," Mr. Calihan growled out as he squeezed one of my breasts, and began to pump into me at a rising pace.

If Russ had ever seen fit to eat me out, or finger me, or just do anything that wasn't selfish, I'd have been his forever. Mr. Calihan barely knew me and he'd taken care of my womanly needs better than I could have imagined. He had gotten me so wet that even with the obscene size of his cock; the pain gave way to pleasure, and I was able to relax back onto the lounge with rolled up eyes.

My mouth was parted, panting as he took me. I offered him up my body willingly, and as he showed his expertise, I was even more eager to serve his whims. His every touch was the perfect mixture of firmness and tenderness, and when he found my mouth, our tongues danced.

Mr. Calihan was a real man. He knew just how to touch me. When to be gentle. When to be rough. When to pull back. When to push me just a bit too far, so I squealed loudly into the beautiful summer air.

"Fuck, you are so damn tight," he groaned out as his pace hit a new high. His thick cock plunging ever so deep into me at a hard pace. His fingers pinched my little pink nipple between two of his knuckles as he kept thrusting away.

We were taking so many risks. The risk that Russ could come and catch us at any moment, the risk of pregnancy, the risk of us barely knowing one another. But I trusted him. It was so weird. Maybe that was just what happened when you lost your virginity. You see who the other person is, and seeing Mr. Calihan was a revelation. Everything in my life, up to that point, had been wrong. Everything I thought I wanted was wrong.

If he knocked me up, if his son caught us, it wouldn't matter.

I wanted this more than I'd ever wanted anything else, and I squealed with raw delight.

And he rewarded me by fucking me harder. This gorgeous older man seemed to know no limits to his stamina as he deflowered me. That thick cock having sundered my maidenhood and just kept barrelling on into me, making me feel bliss like nothing before.

"Cum for Daddy, baby... cum all over my cock," he said to me with such a seductive, gravelly voice.

And I could feel his thick cock twitching and throbbing inside me, eager for that finish too.

Maybe it was his lewd command, or maybe it was just the way he said it. He was a hard man to refuse. I was quickly learning, and my body agreed. Before I'd even fully registered what he said, or how to cum on cue, my pussy tightened around his shaft. My limbs locked up, and I was a spring that was coiled too tight.

A couple of hard thrusts later, and it was all over for me. I screamed, my eyes squeezed shut as my orgasm hit me like a truck. Every part of me spasmed and released, my throat hoarse from the strength of my cries.

And atop me was Mr. Calihan, rocking back and forth as he thrust wildly, his face strained with the intensity of his own pleasure. He grunted and moaned, his cock swelling as he thrust through my orgasm and straight into his own.

That enormous cock just flooding my insides with his thick, rich seed as he let loose a loud, bellowing roar.

"F-fuck! Fuck you're so tight and perfect!" he shouted out as his cock kept spurting that rich cum.

I was holding onto him, my legs and arms wrapped around him in a full body hug. Tears practically leaked out of my eyes from the intensity, and I couldn't catch my breath. I'd never felt something so intense in all my life, and my body quivered with the aftershocks of my orgasm. My pussy milked his cock, desperate for his seed.

My mouth found his shoulder, and I pressed into it, showering his bronzed skin with tiny kisses.

He was slow to stop entirely, but he kissed me, caressed me, and the two of us basked in the moment, savouring the aftermath of my first time. Only after what felt like ages did my eyes open, and I saw it...

There was Russ, standing with his mouth open, staring in shock at his father and me laying in our post-coital bliss.

I couldn't help but grin in triumph at that as I watched him through narrow slits.

"Dad... what the *fuck?!*" Russ bellowed out, sounding more shocked than outraged.

But Mr. Calihan didn't startle or look shaken by the fact we were caught in the act.

"Go away, Russ," he said.

"But you just—"

"What did I say?" Mr. Calihan growled menacingly at his son, and without even raising his voice, I could see how shaken Russ was. That look of fear in his eyes. This was his father. The man who he relied on for all his luxury and wealth.

In that moment, he knew he'd lost me, but risking telling off his dad meant risking everything else. I almost wanted him to push it, for him to blow up his entire life, but he turned tail. His head hung lower as he slunk back into the house, and I couldn't help but giggle.

I thought I'd gotten everything I wanted then, but I had no idea how much better life could get.

The rest of the vacation was amazing. Russ stayed locked up in his room, and Mr. Calihan and I explored so many more things. So many rooms, so many positions. It didn't come as a shock to either of us when, a few months later, the pregnancy test came back positive.

I was true to my word, though, and by then we'd gone on dozens of dates, and visited several countries together. True to his word, he knew how to spoil me rotten, and he taught me things that a guy my age couldn't fathom.

I was a reminder to Russ about what happened when he took things for granted, and honestly, it was for the best. He smartened up a lot after that, and while things were still awkward, he was getting over it. Or at least hiding it better.

As I looked down on the massive ring that Mr. Calihan got me for our engagement, I couldn't help but feel that fate had intervened. Life was *perfect*.

Subscribe for more Candy Quinn:
http://candyquinn.com/newsletter

Recommended For You

For a full list of all my books, or to browse by length or kink, please visit my website!

https://candyquinn.com/books

YOUR NEXT HOT READ

Claimed by My Fiancé's Dad

Spoiled by my Boyfriend's Dad

Stripping for my Boyfriend's Dad

Fertile for My Boyfriend's Dad

Free Exclusive Story
LUST LESSONS: BELLA

She has the hots for teacher

Mr. Wright is totally off limits. Not only is he her teacher, but he's also her brother's best friend.

Bella has never wanted anyone more. At first, she just wants to tease him. She doesn't wear panties, and practically begs him for the big D —- detention — just to prove to him how good she is at being bad. But he wants more than a tease. He wants to claim her fertile, innocent body, and neither of them can resist their forbidden desires.

TEASER

By the time the bell rang and the other students rushed out, Bella's fantasies had her wound up tighter than a knot. Her bare pussy was dripping on her chair, and she slipped out of it eagerly.

"Well, Mr. Wright, you got me alone," she grinned.

Clark gave her a cautionary look, before he went to the door and shut it tight then locked it.

"You really chose an... interesting way to get yourself in trouble, Bella," he said to her as he returned from the door, shaking his head at her in surprised disbelief, a soft chuckle escaping his lips. "But you always were a little terror of a tease," he said as he made his way back towards the class windows, beginning to slide the curtains shut.

"You make it sound so sweet," she giggled, sitting on his desk. She pulled her white skirt out from under her, crossing her legs as she watched him shut the curtains. "I just did what felt natural."

FREE EXCLUSIVE STORY

Get your free copy of Lust Lessons: Bella, and so much more! All you have to do is subscribe to my newsletter.
http://candyquinn.com/newsletter

Become Candy Obsessed

For over a decade, I've been writing the hottest, naughtiest stories I can think of, and I'm addicted. I love to explore the forbidden, the taboo, and the over-the-top sexy. Each story starts off with a sizzle, giving you that nice build up, and that perfect release.

Discover new, secret fantasies, or just indulge in those sticky-sweet guilty pleasures. I'll never judge! Make sure to follow me on your fave site so you never miss a new release.

Plus, if you **sign up for my mailing list**, you'll get updates on my new books, bundles, giveaways, and several **free, exclusive books.**

Connect with Candy!
candyquinn.com
candyquinn.com/newsletter
candy.quinn.erotica@gmail.com

Follow me Everywhere!

- facebook.com/candyquinnromance
- x.com/sexycandyquinn
- amazon.com/Candy-Quinn/e/B00K187NCE
- bookbub.com/authors/candy-quinn

© 2024 Pathforgers Publishing

First published in 2024

All Rights Reserved. No part of this publication may be reproduced, distributed, or transmitted in any form or by any means. If you downloaded an illegal copy of this book and enjoyed it, please buy a legal copy.

This is a work of fiction. Names, characters, business, events and incidents are the products of the author's imagination. Any resemblance to actual persons, living or dead, or actual events is purely coincidental.

This book is intended for sale to Adult Audiences only. All sexually active characters in this work are over 18. All sexual activity is between non-blood related, consenting adults.

Cover Design: Pathforgers Publishing. All cover art makes use of stock photography and all persons depicted are models.